# What is phonics?

Phonics helps children learn to read and write by teaching them the letter sounds (known as phonemes), rather than the letter names, e.g. the sound that 'c' makes rather than its alphabetic name. They then learn how to blend the sounds: the process of saying the sounds in a word or 'sounding out' and then blending them together to make the word, for example c – a – t = cat. Once the phonemes and the skill of blending are learnt, children can tackle reading any phonetically decodable word they come across, even ones they don't know, with confidence and success.

However, there are of course many words in the English language that aren't phonetically decodable, e.g. if a child gets stuck on 'the' it doesn't help if they sound it out and blend it. We call these 'tricky words' and they are just taught as words that are so 'tricky' that children have to learn to recognise them by sight.

# How do phonic readers work?

Phonic reading books are written especially for children who are beginning to learn phonics at nursery or school, and support any programme being used by providing plenty of practice as children develop the skills of decoding and blending. By targeting specific phonemes and tricky words, increasing in difficulty, they ensure systematic progression with reading.

Because phonic readers are primarily decodable – aside from the target tricky words which need to be learnt, children should be able to read the books with real assurance and accomplishment.

# Big Cat phonic readers:
## Ant and Snail

In Big Cat phonic readers the specific phonemes and tricky words being focussed on are highlighted here in these notes, so that you can be clear about what your child's learning and what they need to practise.

While reading at home together, there are all sorts of fun additional games you can play to help your child practise those phonemes and tricky words, which can be a nice way to familiarise yourselves with them before reading, or remind you of them after you've finished. In *Ant and Snail*, for example:

- the focus phonemes are n (run), r (rock), f (fit), ai (snail). Why not write them down and encourage your child to practise saying the sounds as you point to them in a random order. This is called 'Speed Sounds' and as you get faster and faster with your pointing, it encourages your child to say them as quickly as possible. You can try reversing the roles, so that you have a practice too!

- the tricky words are 'the', 'was', 'to' and 'he'. You can play 'Hide and Seek' by asking your child to close their eyes and count to 10, while you write each word on a piece of paper, hiding them somewhere in the room you're in or the garden for your child to find. As they find each one, they should try reading and spelling the word out.

# Reading together

- Have a look at the front cover of *Ant and Snail* and talk about what you can see.

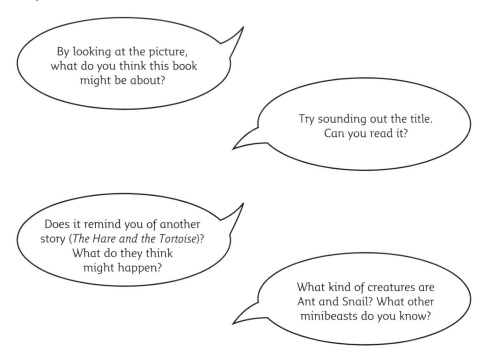

By looking at the picture, what do you think this book might be about?

Try sounding out the title. Can you read it?

Does it remind you of another story (*The Hare and the Tortoise*)? What do they think might happen?

What kind of creatures are Ant and Snail? What other minibeasts do you know?

- Enjoy reading *Ant and Snail* together, noticing the focus phonemes (n, r, f, ai) and tricky words (the, was, to, he). It's useful to point to each word as your child reads, and encouraging to give them lots of praise as they go.

- If your child gets stuck on a word, and it's phonetically decodable, encourage them to sound it out. You can practise blending by saying the sounds aloud a few times, getting quicker and quicker. If they still can't read it, tell them the word and move on.

# Talking about the book

- Use the map on pp18–19 to talk about what happened in the race together.

- Practise the focus phonemes from *Ant and Snail* by asking your child to tell you which sound, for example, the word 'fit' begins with, or how they'd sound out, for example, 'snail'.

# Ant and Snail

Written by Paul Shipton
Illustrated by Jon Stuart

**Collins**

Ant and Snail had a run.

Ant was fit.
Ant was fast.

Snail was not fit.
Snail was not fast.

Ant did not wait for Snail.
He ran off fast.

Ant ran past the big rock.
He did not puff and
he did not pant.

Snail got to the big rock and had a rest.

Ant ran past the grass.
He did not stop.

Ant hit a stick.
He fell in a pit.

Ant was stuck in the pit.

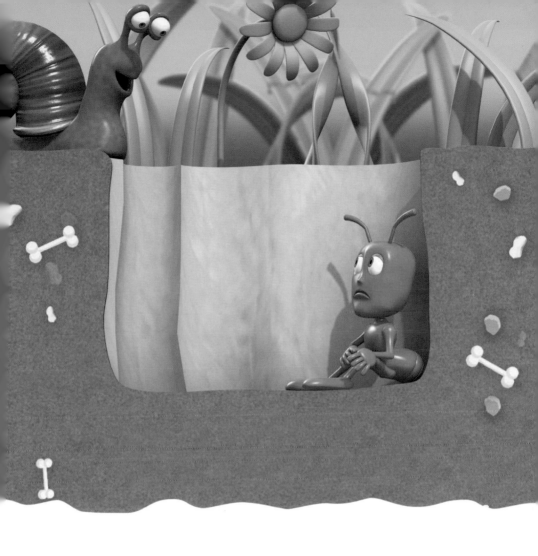

Snail got to the top
of the pit at last.

Snail put the stick in the pit.
Ant ran up it.

Ant and Snail sat on a rock and had a rest.

# A map

rock

grass

stick

pit

# Getting creative

- Have some fun with your child by playing 'Sound Tennis' to practise the focus phonemes, by taking it in turns to mime swinging a bat while saying one of the focus phonemes. Continue until one of you falters!

- To practise the tricky words from the story, why not write them out in bubble writing for your child to decorate and colour. Stick them on the fridge and practise them regularly.

- If your child's enjoyed reading *Ant and Snail* maybe they could research other minibeasts, using books or the internet.

- Why not go on a bug hunt in the garden or local park to see what minibeasts you can find.

# Other books at Level I:

| Fiction | Non-fiction |
|---|---|
| Sam and the Nut — Cheryl Webster, Giuditta Gaviraghi | Got It! — Charlotte Guillain, Leo Hartas-Roberts |
| We Are Not Fond of Rat! — Emma Chichester Clark | Pet Cat, Big Cat — Alison Hawes |
| Ant and Snail — Paul Shipton, Jon Stuart | Pond Food — John Townsend, Pamela Anzalotti |

Published by Collins
An imprint of HarperCollins*Publishers*
1 London Bridge Street
London
SE1 9GF

Author: Paul Shipton

British Library Cataloguing in Publication Data
A catalogue record for this publication is available from the British Library.

Illustrator: Jon Stuart
Designer: Niki Whitehorn, niki@whitehorndesign.co.nz
Parent notes authors: Sue Reed and Liz Webster

Printed and bound by RR Donnelley APS

www.collins.co.uk/parents